YOU'RE NOT A PROPER PIRATE, SIDNEY GREEN!

For Charlie – R. Q.
For Finn – D. A.

First published 2019 by Nosy Crow Ltd
The Crow's Nest, 14 Baden Place, Crosby Row, London SE1 1YW • www.nosycrow.com
ISBN 978 1 78800 200 4 (HB) • ISBN 978 1 78800 201 1 (PB)
Nosy Crow and associated logos are trademarks and/or registered trademarks of Nosy Crow Ltd
Text © Ruth Quayle 2019 • Illustrations © Deborah Allwright 2019
The right of Ruth Quayle to be identified as the author and Deborah Allwright to be identified
as the illustrator of this work has been asserted. • All rights reserved.

Printed in China • Papers used by Nosy Crow are made from wood grown in sustainable forests.
1 3 5 7 9 8 6 4 2 (HB) • 1 3 5 7 9 8 6 4 2 (PB)

You're NOT A PROPER PIRATE, SIDNEY GREEN!

Ruth Quayle & Deborah Allwright

nosy crow

On an ordinary day way back in history, like 4 or 5 or 19 weeks ago, Sidney Green and his dog, Jemima, were just playing, when . . .

a letter arrived.

The letter said:

Dear Sidney Green,

You have spent too long just playing. It's time to become a proper pirate. Please report to me immediately.

Yours heartily,

Captain
Shipshape

"Being a proper pirate sounds like fun,"
Sidney Green told Jemima. "But first we
need to compete in a Very Important Race."
So he wrote a quick note back to Captain Shipshape:
"I'll come in a minute."

And – whoosh . . .

They zoomed along at more than 150 miles per hour, zipped around corners,

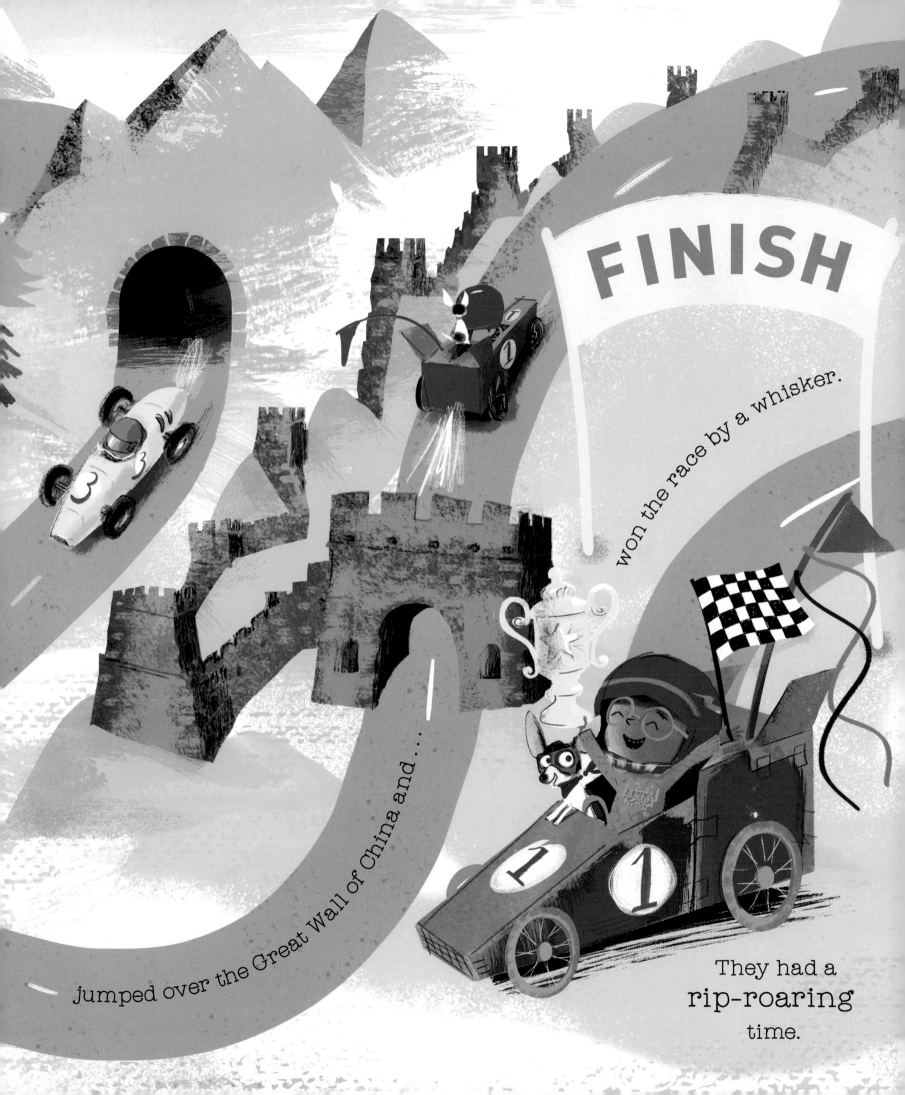

FINISH

won the race by a whisker.

jumped over the Great Wall of China and . . . .

They had a
rip-roaring
time.

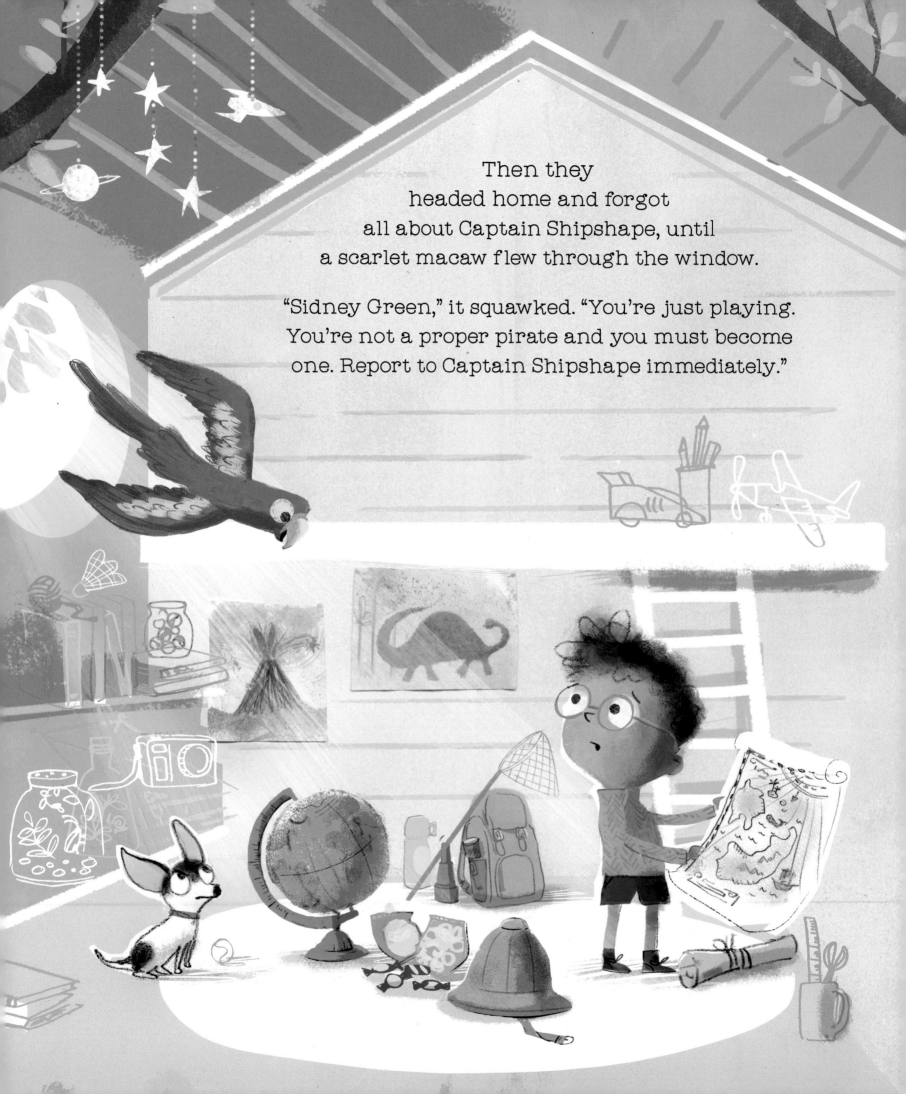

Then they
headed home and forgot
all about Captain Shipshape, until
a scarlet macaw flew through the window.

"Sidney Green," it squawked. "You're just playing.
You're not a proper pirate and you must become
one. Report to Captain Shipshape immediately."

"I'll come in a minute," said Sidney Green,
"but we're just in the middle of a Very
Important Expedition."

"Oooh," said the scarlet macaw.
"That sounds exciting. Can I join in?"

So they all set off for Africa . . .

They got lost
in the ocean,

tumbled down a waterfall,

nearly got eaten by a shark, but arrived in Africa just in time ... for a hippo's birthday party. They had a **rip-roaring** time.

Then they went home and forgot all about Captain Shipshape, until there was a loud knock on the door.

"Sidney Green," said three smart pirates with shiny cutlasses. "You're just playing. You're not a proper pirate and you must become one. Report to Captain Shipshape **immediately.**"

"I'll come in a minute," said Sidney Green, "but we're just in the middle of a Very Important Building Project."

"Hmmm," said the pirates.
"That looks interesting.
Can we join in?"

So they all started to build
an enormous castle . . .

It had . . .

23 turrets,

17 dungeons

and a moat full of crocodiles.

They had a **rip-roaring** time.

Back home, they were just cooling off with a glass of lemonade, when . . .

Captain Shipshape himself arrived.

"You're NOT a proper
pirate, Sidney Green!"
roared Captain Shipshape.
"You're just playing!
We have so much to do
and so little time. I need
to keep my ship shipshape.

You MUST become a proper
pirate right now because . . .

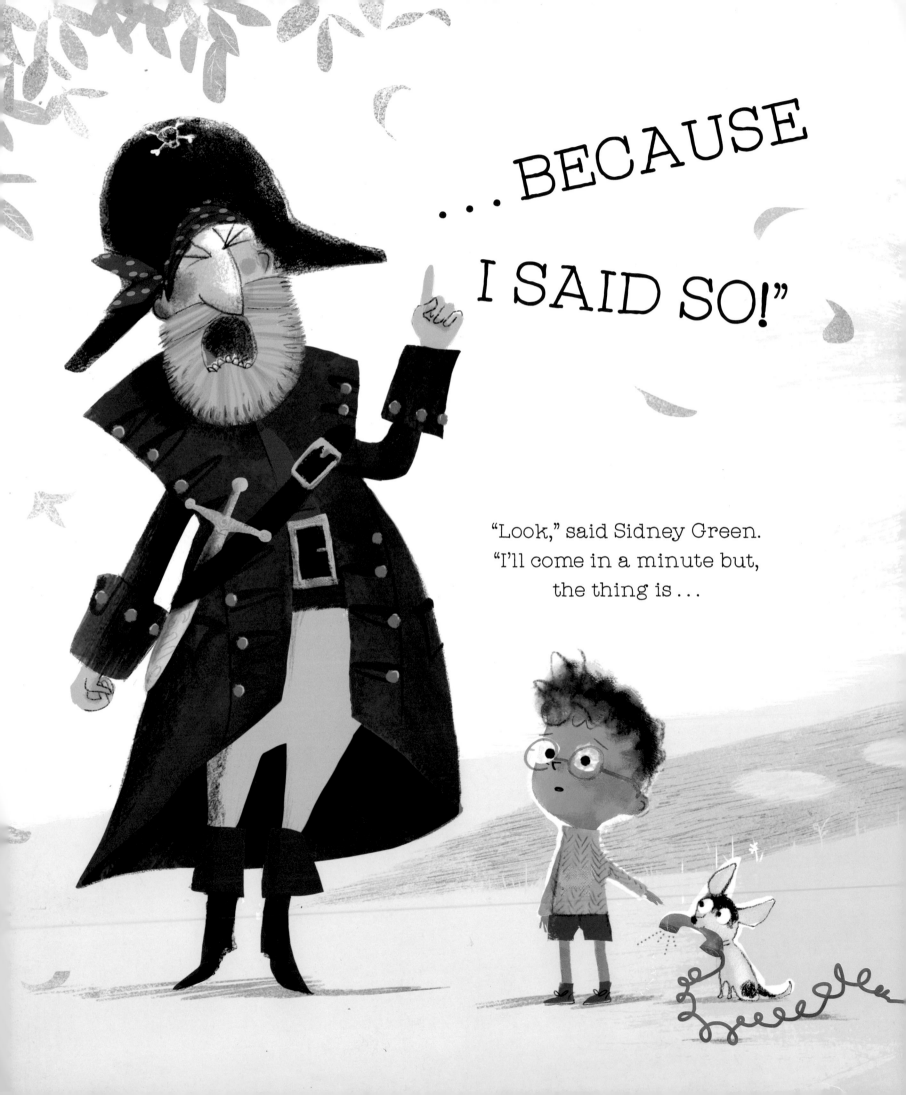

...BECAUSE I SAID SO!"

"Look," said Sidney Green.
"I'll come in a minute but,
the thing is ...

I've just received a Very Important Phone Call.
Aliens are planning to attack Earth and we
need to stop them."

Captain Shipshape turned bright red.
He opened his mouth to start shouting
again, when . . .

DONK!

. . . a piece of flying moon rock
landed on his head.

"Wait for me!"
cried Captain Shipshape.

"Well," said Sidney Green. "If you're going to be in my crew, I think you'd better wear a space helmet too."

So they all fastened their helmets securely.

Then they blasted into outer space . . .

tracked down the dangerous aliens . . .

and chased them back to
a far and distant planet.

And they all had
an absolutely
RIP-ROARING
time.

Back home, they were just having a rest
in Sidney Green's sandpit, when ...

Mrs Shipshape arrived.

"Captain Shipshape," she called.
"You're just playing! Cabin boy Jim has
made your tea. Wash your hands and
come right now, please."

Captain Shipshape looked at Sidney Green and grinned.
"OK," he said. "But we're just in the middle of a Very
Important Dinosaur Dig ...

. . . I'll come in a minute!"

So they turned on their torches, picked up their best digging tools and . . .

"You've done it! You've found the treasure!"
said Captain Shipshape.

"You're a proper pirate,
Sidney Green!"